Live the Dream!

White Wolves Series Consultant: Sue Ellis,
Centre for Literacy in Primary Education

This book can be used in the White Wolves Guided Reading programme with children who have an average level of reading experience at Year 4 level.

First published 2004 by
A & C Black Publishers Ltd
37 Soho Square, London, W1D 3QZ

www.acblack.com

ISBN 0-7136-6862-8

A CIP catalogue for this book is available from the British Library.

A&C Black uses paper produced with elemental chlorine-free pulp, harvested from managed sustained forests.

Printed and bound in Spain by G. Z. Printek, Bilbao.

Live the Dream!

by Jenny Oldfield
illustrated by Jennie Maizels

A & C Black • London

Contents

Surfing

"Where's Zoey?"

"In her room."

"What's she up to?"

"Leave her alone, she's surfing."

Zoey heard but didn't pay any attention. She was busy clicking her mouse, pressing keys, having a great time.

Internet Explorer
Dial-up connection

7

Select the service you want to connect to, and then enter your username and password.

Zoey typed the word "zillion" and waited.

The computer beeped and whirred. Soon it invited her to connect.

Dialling ...
Dialling attempt 1 ...
Dialling ...

This was wicked. Zoey always got a buzz from watching the screen flash up its colourful commands and listening to the machine's innards squeak.

Eek-errk-rrr!

She clicked the mouse on the search box and typed in the word "dream".

This was what she was in the mood for doing – nothing too hard, nothing that asked her to think or win. No, just dreaming would be fine! Live the dream.

Come in and see how easy it is to make your dreams come true.

Click-click, she entered the site.

Chapter One

Type in the keyword to your favourite fantasy.

Zoey grinned and typed "princess".

A picture came up on screen of a girl in a silver dress and sequinned shoes. The speakers played the soundtrack to Disney's *Cinderella*.

Do you really want to be a princess?

... the machine asked.

And live in a palace, be driven around in a flash car, meet Prince Charming?

"Yes." Zoey typed her reply in the empty box.

Sure? But what if Prince Charming turned out to be Prince Geek, and you had to have bodyguards everywhere you went, and they kept on printing nasty pictures of you in "Hello" magazine?

"No," Zoey typed. And the girl in the silver dress faded from the screen.

Type in the keyword to your favourite fantasy.

… the computer invited her a second time.

OK, so not princess. How about "supermodel"?

s–u–p–e–r–m–o–d–e–l

A picture came up of a stick-thin girl in a mini-skirt and skinny-top. She was strutting her stuff on the catwalk while the speakers played loud, funky music.

Do you really want to be a supermodel?

"No." Wow, no way. What *had* she been thinking?

She would have to spend hours having her kinky hair straightened and dyed, her legs waxed, her face made up. And all that time she could have been chatting with her mates or having a game of footie in the back garden.

Or even surfing the net – *yeah!*

Type in the keyword to your favourite fantasy.

This time Zoey went for "cowgirl". The idea flashed into her head – she didn't know where it came from.

"Yee-hah!" the speakers blared, with banjo music jangling away in the background. The girl on screen wore a white stetson and a wide grin. She was carrying a lasso.

Do you really want
to be a cowgirl?

"Yeah!" All those neat horses with big saddles and long stirrups. All that galloping through mountain passes whirling your lasso!

A new picture came up of the same girl herding black and white cows into a dusty corral. The cows looked dead miserable. The girl looked dirty and tired.

Do you wish to continue?

"Yes." This time Zoey was less sure. And when a pic came up of the cows being shoved down metal chutes and loaded on to a truck, she changed her mind and said, "No."

The cowgirl faded. Ah well, another dream had bitten the dust!

Type in the keyword.

Yeah, yeah! Off the top of her head she tried "astronaut" and then "racing car driver", but the computer was getting smarter.

Do you wish to continue?
… it asked. And …

Is this your deepest wish?
Then …

Check your last answer.
Are you sure you want
to go ahead?

"Hey, don't get pushy with me!" Zoey muttered. It was weird, but the machine seemed to know that she wasn't telling the truth.

"You're just a hard disk and a set of microchips, OK?"

This is your last chance!
... the computer argued back.

Type in the keyword to your favourite fantasy.

Chapter Two

"Dolphin," Zoey typed.

She'd had to dig deep for this one. After all, she was Zoey Williams, aged nine, with a baby brother called Al, a mum and a step-dad. She went to Ridgeway Junior School with her best mate, Rosanna. Kids like her didn't get to swim with dolphins.

Do you really want to be a dolphin?

… the computer asked.

Not *be* a dolphin, stupid! I want to swim with them! She typed the word "swim" then waited.

Do you wish to continue?

Do I? She wondered. I mean, life is pretty cool as it is, thanks. OK, so Al wakes the whole house up in the middle of the night with his yelling and squawking, and he's messy from both ends – yuck.

And OK, my real dad has moved to Scotland and I only get to see him one weekend every two months. But I have a nice life, I really do.

Do you wish to continue?
... the box flashed impatiently.

"Yes, please," she typed politely.

Check your last answer.

Do you want to go ahead?

Look, I'm telling you I want to swim with dolphins, OK! You're asking me to tell you my favourite fantasy, and I'm doing the best I can!

The computer whirred and clicked, then it flashed up a new box ...

Answer validated. Where do you want to go?

"I want to go where there are dolphins – doh!"

Water World - near Hull?

24

"No, I'd like to see them in the wild."

OK, how about Zanzibar?

Zanzi-what? Where on earth was that? "Tell me more," she typed.

Click-whirr-beep!

Zanzibar is a spice island off the coast of Africa. It has palm trees and clear blue seas. Do you wish to continue?

Zoey's heart raced. She pictured white waves breaking on to golden sands, and only her, Zoey Williams, on the whole, empty beach.

"You bet!" she typed.

Chapter Three

Zoey had dreamed this dream
since she was seven. It was to
get into a small wooden boat and
row out to sea. The sea was deep
blue – you could see the sandy
bottom.

Overhead there was a hot, hot
sun. Shoals of silver fish swam up
to the boat. You could reach out
and run your fingers through the
clear water.

Soon you came to the place where the dolphins swam. They cruised towards you with lazy flicks of their tails, pushing their blunt noses out of the water and making funny squeaking sounds. *Eek-erk-urk-urk!* They had small, dead intelligent eyes.

"Come in!" they seemed to say. "It's great in here!"

In her dream, Zoey would
stand up and the small boat would
wobble. She would fling her arms
wide like a tightrope walker, find
her balance, then edge towards
the side of the boat. It tipped and
rocked. She would raise her arms
above her head like a high-diver.

But there was no sploosh, no diving into the fishy world. The dream would end and she would wake up on dry land, snug in her own bed.

Are you sure that this is your favourite fantasy?

"Yes, yes, yes!" Zoey typed. But she deliberately wasn't telling the computer one important fact.

To swim with dolphins?

How many times – yes!!!

Whine-whirr-click-beep!

Live your dreams! the computer said. **Press enter.**

Zoey pressed "Enter".

She was in a small wooden boat, but she wasn't alone. There was a dark-skinned boy rowing it, dressed in faded denim shorts. The big oars looked too heavy for his skinny arms.

Zoey held on to the sides of the
boat. They bobbed up and down
on the waves rolling on to the
shore. Behind them, the beach was
fringed with tall palm trees, and
behind the trees there was a forest
and then mountains. She looked
down at her own bare feet, then up
and out to sea.

The boy rowed. The oars splashed in and out of the water.

I'm here! Zoey thought. It's really happening – wow!

It must be real – she could feel the hot sun on her back, the boy was smiling and babbling in a language she didn't understand.

And then there were the fish – the little ones, just like in her dreams, flashing silver, swimming in huge shoals close to the surface.

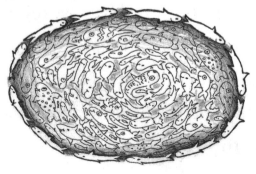

The boy pointed to the distant
horizon – a flat line between the
sky and the sea.

Zoey nodded. He was telling
her that the dolphins were out
there – lots of them – a whole
school. She didn't know how she
knew this, but she did.

Here she was, Zoey Williams, aged nine (and a half), dressed in a swimming costume and a flowery sarong thingy, with bare feet, rowing with a stranger in a foreign land.

Out there were her favourite creatures of all time – better than dogs and cats, better, even, than horses. Out there were dolphins!

Chapter Four

It was pretty scary, though.

The waves rose and fell, they broke with a rush of foam that sprayed up into your face and dried in a salty crust on your skin.

The boy flashed a smile as Zoey held tight and clenched her teeth. Soon they were past the breakers and out on the smooth ocean. The small fish followed them, like silver leaves.

A million round, fishy eyes stared up at them.

"How long before we see the dolphins?" Zoey asked.

He grinned and pulled at the oars.

"Oh yeah – I forgot," she murmured. He didn't speak English.

After a while she got used to being in the boat. She leaned out to trail her fingers in the water.

The tiny fish darted away. When she lifted her arm, it was wet and slippery in the sun, like an eel.

The boy stopped rowing and handed her a slice of melon. The flesh was red, the skin green. She ate it and spat out the black pips. He chattered at her, she smiled back at him.

"Zoey!" she said, patting her chest.

"Jusef!" he replied.

Jusef: in his faded, baggy shorts, arms and legs like sticks, feet placed either side of hers in the bottom of the boat.

If you rowed for ever, you would never reach the horizon, she decided.

Jusef stopped and let the boat drift. It was a tiny speck in the blue, sparkling sea.

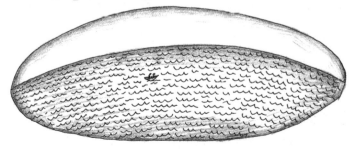

"Are they here?" Zoey asked, leaning out over the side.

She gazed down into the water. The longer you looked, the more it seemed more green than blue. It lapped the sides of the boat with a small, clean slap.

They drifted for ages before she saw them. The sun had shone, they were miles from land.

"There!" she cried.

Jusef smiled and nodded.

The first dolphin rose from the depths – a pale, shimmering shape heading for the surface. He bobbed clear of the water then dived out of sight – just long enough for Zoey to point and cry out a second time.

"He's fast!" she gasped.

Then dolphins Number Two and Three popped up on the other side of the boat. One flicked his tail, the other rolled over to show his white belly.

"Hah!" Zoey said.

Number Three rolled and dipped under the water.

"Wow, cool!"

Number One came back and did some jiggling about by the boat. She could see his blunt, beak-like nose and little serrated teeth, hear the clack of his jaws as he snapped them shut.

"Hi to you too!" she grinned.

Jusef laughed out loud. He stood up and mimed diving into the water, bending his knees and doing a cartoon dive without actually leaving the boat.

Zoey gasped. "Oh, no!" She cowered away from him, shaking her head. "I'll just sit here for a bit!"

By now the place was alive with dolphins. They surged up from the green depths and leaped clear of the surface, raising their silver-grey bodies in graceful arcs before splashing back into the sea.

They came in twos and threes,
having contests to see who could
jump highest and fastest. They
trailed spray after them and
showered Zoey with a million
diamond drops mined from the
ocean.

Then they plunged under the
boat, making it rock. They came
up again, rolling, twisting and
flicking their broad tails.

"Magic!" Zoey breathed through her fear.

They were beautiful beyond her dreams.

Jusef stood there and did his funny miming dive twice and then three times.

"No!" she protested, holding up her palms and pretending to push him away.

The boy laughed, bent his knees, and this time dived into the water for real.

Zoey panicked as he vanished from sight. "Come back!"

He reappeared, riding the back of a dolphin, holding on to its flippers, yelling with delight. The dolphin bore him through the waves.

And she wanted to dive in after him. She longed to be lifted by one of these strong creatures, to tear through the water like a tanned surfer on a board.

But she couldn't.

This was the part she'd deliberately kept secret from the computer.

Jusef let go of the dolphin, sank into the water and and waved her in.

"I can't!" she whispered, sitting there and feeling the boat rock.

The land was miles away, the glittering horizon went on for ever.

And it came out in a rush – the silly, ginormous secret that she'd been hiding all this time.

"I can't swim!"

Chapter Five

There was the time at Ridgeway Leisure Centre when she'd been standing by the deep end of the pool without her stupid water wings.

A kid had rushed by and shoved her in. She remembered the cold shock of the water, the panic when her feet didn't touch the bottom.

Gurgle-gurgle-gulp.

She'd swallowed loads of water before she'd bobbed back to the top. She'd coughed and spluttered and waved her arms around until someone's mum had seen her and scooped her out. She'd only been five years old.

Since then, swimming was a big no-no. When you're five and you can't breathe, it scares the heck out of you.

"I can't swim!" she told Jusef, putting her hands to her throat and miming choking to death. *Glug-glug.*

Live your dream!

He laughed and surged backwards through the water, flicking over into a back-flip and coming up all smiles. Two dolphins came and nudged him from behind.

"I'll drown!" she warned. The green sea was deeper than any pool.

Other dolphins swam up and creak-clacked in a language of their own. *Come in, the water's great! It's a breeze!*

"I can't. I'm scared!"

Come in. We won't let

you drown. They flipped and twisted, rolled and turned.

Zoey felt the boat wobble and gazed down at the acrobats of the sea.

She thought, Yeah, I can do that! And jumped in.

Her feet didn't touch the bottom. She plunged down among the dolphins and the bubbles, spiralling, twisting, keeping her eyes wide open.

A dolphin came close and swam alongside. Zoey reached out her hand and grabbed his flipper. He felt smooth and firm, not slimy. His eyes and mouth seemed to smile. Hold tight!

She saw shadowy shapes of other dolphins, skinny Jusef diving down to watch her, flat fish and round fish, fish with long, trailing tails.

Wonderful! Mega! Magic!

Then her dolphin tilted his nose upwards and took her to the surface.

She broke clear of the water and gulped in air, clung to her dolphin's back and took a ride around the ocean.

This is cool, right? *Erk-erk-urk.*

Cool to see the distant palm trees and white beach, the shimmer of heat on the sand. The empty boat bobbed nearby.

You're safe – you can stop holding on now.

And Zoey knew she could let go and float. She was by herself, lying on her back like a cork, staring up at the blue sky.

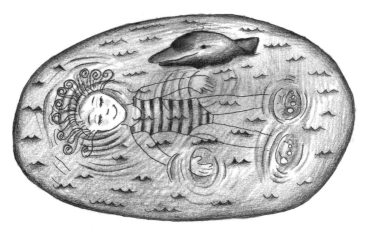

Say that again – floating!

She kicked her legs and paddled with her arms. Swimming even!

Her dolphin stayed by her, just in case.

Zoey turned on to her front and tried out a couple of strokes. Jusef was laughing. The dolphins rolled and flicked their tails.

She, Zoey Williams, was swimming with dolphins!

Logging Off

You are working online. Do you want to stay connected?

"Yes."

If she logged off, the dolphins would disappear. No more Jusef, no more spice island.

Click here to continue.

Zoey clicked. The screen showed a picture of three dolphins leaping out of the sea, but she wasn't on it.

Are you sure you want to stay connected?

There was a noise in her head of waves breaking, foam splashing, and in the distance, Jusef laughing. But the sound was fading.

"Yes," she typed.

For a few moments longer she could feel the sea spray and the sensation of her body buoyed up in the clear water. Then this too began to disappear.

You have lived your dream.

… the computer told her.

How cool was that? *Very* cool.

Are you ready to disconnect now?

She hesitated. The last thing she heard was the call of the dolphins. "Yes," she said.

"Zoey!" Mum called.

Click here. Back to Search.

She watched the graphics flick and change until her screensaver reappeared. It was a picture of a dolphin leaping out of a blue sea.

Hmm, how did that get there?

"Zoey!" Mum came up the stairs. "Rosanna's on the phone. Do you want to go round to her place?"

Windows is shutting down.

"Yeah – cool," Zoey said.

"Have you logged off?"

"Yep."

She left the computer sitting quietly on her desk.

No signal.

Until next time.

About the Author

Jenny Oldfield was born in Yorkshire, where she still lives with her two daughters, Kate and Eve. She read English at university and then pursued a number of jobs before she started writing at the age of twenty-four. She has now published over fifty books for adults and children, many in popular series including *Horses of Half-Moon Ranch* and *Definitely Daisy*. Jenny has always loved the outdoors and when she isn't writing, she loves horse riding, playing tennis, walking and travelling to far-off places.

Other White Wolves titles you might enjoy ...

Hugo and the Long Red Arm by **Rachel Anderson**

When Hugo breaks his arm, he thinks he'll be bored and useless. But with his mum's new reaching, grabbing and twirling invention, Hugo's world is turned upside down!

Swan Boy by **Diana Hendry**

How did Caleb turn into a creature part boy and part swan, and come to live alone on the island of Nanna? Find out in this haunting story.

White Wolves